ANNIE PAT and EDDIE

By the Same Author

Published by William Morrow and Company

ANNIE PAT AND EDDIE. 1960

EDDIE AND LOUELLA. 1959

BETSY'S WINTERHOUSE. 1958

EDDIE MAKES MUSIC. 1957

BETSY'S BUSY SUMMER. 1956

EDDIE AND HIS BIG DEALS. 1955

BETSY AND THE CIRCUS. 1954

EDDIE'S PAY DIRT. 1953

THE MIXED-UP TWINS. 1952

EDDIE AND GARDENIA. 1951

BETSY'S LITTLE STAR. 1950

EDDIE AND THE FIRE ENGINE. 1949

PENNY GOES TO CAMP. 1948

LITTLE EDDIE. 1947

Published by Harcourt, Brace and Company

PENNY AND PETER. 1946

BETSY AND THE BOYS. 1945

HERE'S A PENNY. 1944

BACK TO SCHOOL WITH BETSY. 1943

PRIMROSE DAY. 1942

BETSY AND BILLY. 1941

TWO AND TWO ARE FOUR. 1940

"B" IS FOR BETSY. 1939

ANNIE PAT and EDDIE

Written and illustrated by
CAROLYN HAYWOOD

New York, 1960
WILLIAM MORROW & COMPANY

J

Third Printing, September, 1962

Library of Congress Catalog Card Number 60-11077

To
Helen Appleton
with my love

CONTENTS

ANNIE PAT and EDDIE

CHAPTER 1

ACTRESSES HAVE RED HAIR

Iт was the last week in June. In five more days school would close and the summer vacation would begin. Some of the children were going away to camp. Some were going to the seashore. Others, like Eddie Wilson, were going to visit relatives who lived far away, but many of the boys and girls were staying at home.

Of all the children, Eddie was the most excited, because he was going back to his uncle's ranch in Texas. But one morning Anna Patricia Wallace arrived at school more excited than Eddie had ever been. She rushed up to Eddie and said, "Do you know what, Eddie Wilson?"

"What?" said Eddie.

"I'm going to be an actress," said Anna Patricia.

"So what?" said Eddie.

"So what!" exclaimed Anna Patricia. "It's fabulous."

"You can't be an actress," said Eddie.

"I should like to know why not!"

" 'Cause you don't have red hair," said Eddie.

"What has that got to do with it?" asked Anna Patricia, but she didn't sound quite so bouncy as she had.

"All actresses have red hair," said Eddie, and he began to name one after another, checking them off on his fingers.

When he had finished, Anna Patricia said, "There are lots of actresses who don't have red hair."

14

"Who?" said Eddie.

Anna Patricia wrinkled up her forehead and thought. She couldn't think of one actress who did not have red hair. Finally she said, "Well, I can't think of any right now, but I know there are some."

"Didn't I tell you?" said Eddie. "You can't be an actress with that hair. It isn't any color at all."

"Why, Eddie Wilson!" exclaimed Anna Patricia. "What do you mean, my hair isn't any color at all? If it wasn't any color at all it would be white, and my hair isn't white. It's blond."

"Well, blond isn't any color," said Eddie. "Did you ever have any paint that was called blond? It isn't a color, I tell you. It isn't red or black or brown or green or blue or purple. It isn't even yellow."

"Eddie Wilson!" cried Anna Patricia. "I don't want green or blue or purple hair."

"Well, you haven't got it," said Eddie. "It's just blond."

15

Anna Patricia felt like a limp balloon, but she said, "It's curly."

"Yes," said Eddie, "but it's no good for being an actress if it isn't red."

The bell rang for school to begin and Anna Patricia hadn't had a chance to tell Eddie how she was going to be an actress. All they had talked about was her hair and how it wasn't red. That was just like Eddie. Whenever she wanted to talk about something, he always talked about something else.

It was time for the arithmetic lesson now, but Anna Patricia took hold of one of her curls and looked at it out of the corner of her eye. She held it up and she held it down. It did not look red. She held it in a ray of sunlight. Anna Patricia thought it looked a little like gold in the sunlight, but it did not look red.

"Anna Patricia," said her teacher, "what are you doing?"

"Trying to see if my hair looks red," replied Anna Patricia.

"It isn't," said Miss Ross, "so don't try any longer. Pay attention to your arithmetic lesson."

Anna Patricia had a hard time paying attention to the arithmetic lesson, because she wanted so much to tell everyone about how she was going to be an actress. Finally, when she had answered, "Seven," to Miss Ross's question, "How much is thirty-six divided by four," her teacher said, "Anna Patricia, what is the matter with you this morning?"

"I guess it's because I'm going to be an actress," Anna Patricia replied.

"Well, even actresses have to know how to do arithmetic," said Miss Ross. Anna Patricia pulled her mind off being an actress and paid attention to the arithmetic lesson. Next time she was able to give the correct answer.

At recess, Anna Patricia was in the center of a

group of girls. "I'm going to be an actress this summer," she said.

"Where are you going to be an actress this summer?" asked her friend, Carol.

"I'm going to a place at the seashore where a friend of Mother's has a Children's Theater," Anna Patricia replied. "Her name is Mrs. Wells."

"You're making this up," said Carol. "You never told us about your mother's friend before."

"I never wanted to be an actress before," said Anna Patricia.

"Oh!" said Carol.

"Eddie Wilson says I can't be an actress 'cause I don't have red hair," said Anna Patricia.

"You can make it red," said Carol. "My mother's hairdresser gave her a sample of something to make her hair red."

"What is it?" asked Anna Patricia.

"It comes in a bottle," Carol replied. "My mother

gave it to me because she thought my daddy might not like her to have red hair. She says I can use some on my doll's hair and make it red."

"When are you going to use it on your doll's hair?" Anna Patricia asked.

"Maybe I'll do it this afternoon," said Carol. Then Carol's face lighted up and she said, "Why don't you come over to my house after school and you can watch me do it?"

"All right," said Anna Patricia, as the bell rang for the children to return to their classrooms.

When Anna Patricia reached home after school, she found her mother measuring material for new curtains. "Mother," said Anna Patricia, "may I go over to Carol's?"

"Yes, you can go over to Carol's," said her mother.

"Mother," said Anna Patricia, "would you like my hair if it was red?"

Her mother went right on measuring the material.

21

"Three yards, four yards, five yards," she counted off.

"Would you, Mother?" said Anna Patricia.

"Six yards," said her mother. "I would like you with any color hair, darling. Seven yards."

"Eddie Wilson says actresses have red hair and I can't be an actress unless I have red hair too," said Anna Patricia.

"Nonsense!" said her mother. "Eight yards. I knew an actress once who didn't have any hair at all. She wore a wig."

"Do you think I would look nice with red hair, Mother?" said Anna Patricia.

"Eight yards and twenty-four inches," her mother muttered, and stuck a pin into the material.

"Do you, Mother?" said Anna Patricia.

"Don't bother me, Anna Patricia, when I'm measuring," said Mrs. Wallace.

"Well, do you?" said Anna Patricia.

"Yes, yes, of course," said her mother.

"Good-by, Mother," said Anna Patricia. "I'm going to help Carol dye her doll's hair red."

"Be home by half past five," said her mother, as she tore off a strip of material.

When Anna Patricia arrived at Carol's house, she found Carol in the bathroom, undressing her doll. "The stuff is ready to do her hair," said Carol. "It's in that basin."

Anna Patricia looked into the basin. "It isn't red," she said. "It looks like milk."

"Well, I guess it turns red when it gets on your hair," said Carol.

"Are you sure it won't hurt your doll's hair?" said Anna Patricia.

Carol laughed. "Of course not. The hairdresser gave it to my mother," she said, and she stuck her doll's yellow head into the basin.

"It isn't turning red," said Anna Patricia, looking over Carol's shoulder.

"It will," said Carol. "You have to sop it good."

Carol sopped it, while Anna Patricia watched. Finally Anna Patricia said, "My mother said she thinks I would look nice with red hair."

"She did?" said Carol. "How about if I do yours when I finish Gloria's?"

"Let's wait and see how Gloria looks first," said Anna Patricia.

Carol held Gloria up by the legs and squeezed the liquid out of her hair. Gloria's hair looked like a wet paintbrush. "I'll lay her on the window sill in the sun to dry," said Carol. "Will you spread a newspaper on the window sill, please, Anna Patricia?"

Anna Patricia spread the newspaper on the window sill, and Carol laid her doll down and spread her hair out behind her head. Then she turned to Anna Patricia and said, "Now why don't you let me do yours, while that stuff in the basin is nice and fresh?"

"I would like to see how Gloria's looks first," said Anna Patricia.

"You can't tell anything from Gloria's," said Carol, "because Gloria's hair is a different color from your hair. Gloria's hair is yellow."

"Well, I know that," said Anna Patricia. "But I should like to see, anyway."

"Anna Patricia!" said Carol. "If you don't let me do yours right away, it won't be dry by the time you have to go home."

"Oh, all right!" said Anna Patricia. "I guess I had better take off my dress. I don't want to get spots on it."

She took off her dress. Then she hung her head over the basin and her curls fell in.

Carol picked up a small glass. She dipped it into the basin and poured the milky liquid over Anna Patricia's head until all of her hair was wet. "Now," said

Carol, "you just stay that way for a minute. I want to see how Gloria looks."

"Well, hurry up!" said Anna Patricia, her face muffled in a washcloth. "I don't want this stuff to get in my eyes."

Carol went to the window sill and looked at Gloria. She took just one look and then she cried, "Oh! Gloria's hair!"

"What's the matter with it?" Anna Patricia called back.

"It's all melted!" said Carol. "She hasn't any hair at all! It's gone!" Just then the telephone bell rang. "Oh, dear!" said Carol. "I'll have to see who that is. Maybe it's my mother. She went to the market."

"No! No!" cried Anna Patricia. "Get this off my hair. Get it off!"

"I have to answer the telephone," said Carol, running out of the room and down the stairs.

Anna Patricia's head was already out of the basin.

26

Now she turned on the faucet in the bathtub and kicked off her shoes at the same time. Then she stepped into the tub without taking time to undress. She lay down in the tub on her stomach and stuck her head under the running water. When Carol returned, Anna Patricia shouted above the noise of the running water, "Soap! Soap! Soap!"

Carol picked up a package of soapflakes that was standing on the floor. She shook them all over Anna Patricia's head. "Poor Gloria!" said Carol. "Poor Gloria!"

"Oh! What will my mother say! What will my mother say!" Anna Patricia moaned, as she rubbed soapflakes into a lather.

"That was your mother on the telephone," said Carol.

"What did she want?" Anna Patricia asked, smothered in soapsuds.

"She said you were not to even think of dyeing your hair," replied Carol.

"What did you say?" said Anna Patricia.

"I said 'Poor Gloria's hair is all melted.'"

"Oh!" cried Anna Patricia. "More soap! More soap!"

Carol poured more soapflakes over Anna Patricia's head. "You're using up all of my mother's soapflakes," said Carol. "And how are you ever going to go home in those wet clothes?"

"I don't care about my clothes," said Anna Patricia, rubbing her head harder. "I just don't want my hair to melt."

"Oh, poor Gloria!" said Carol.

Just then Carol's mother returned. She came up-stairs and into the bathroom. "What on earth are you doing?" she said, when she saw Anna Patricia in the bathtub.

"Carol put some stuff on my hair to make it red like

30

an actress," said Anna Patricia. "It melted Gloria's!"

"Oh, Mother!" said Carol. "Look at poor Gloria!"

"I think I had better look at poor Anna Patricia," said Carol's mother, leaning over the bathtub.

"What did you use, Carol?" her mother asked.

"Well, Mother, you said I could use that hair stuff on Gloria. The stuff the hairdresser gave you. I got it out of this bottle. The label is torn."

Carol held up the bottle. Her mother looked at it. "That's the wrong bottle! That's paint remover!" she said.

"Oh!" screamed Anna Patricia. "Is it removing all my hair?"

"Poor Gloria!" said Carol, with a deep sigh.

"I don't think it is," said Carol's mother. "I think you've probably washed it all out. Now let's get you dried off and into some dry clothes."

Anna Patricia stepped out of the tub dripping. Carol's mother went to get some clothes for Anna Patricia to put on, for the only thing that was dry was Anna Patricia's dress.

When she came back, she rubbed Anna Patricia's hair with a towel to dry it. Anna Patricia kept saying, "Is it coming out? Is it coming out?"

Carol's mother kept saying, "No, it isn't coming out," and Carol kept saying, "Poor Gloria!"

With the help of an electric hand dryer, Anna Patricia was soon looking like herself again. At a little before half past five she went home, carrying her damp clothes in a shopping bag. When she reached home, she told her mother all about what had happened.

"And do you know, Mother?" she said. "All Carol could say was 'Poor Gloria.'"

"Anna Patricia," said her mother, when she had heard the whole story, "don't ever do anything to your hair again. It's very nice, just as it is."

The following day, when Anna Patricia went to

school, she rushed up to Eddie and said, "Oh, Eddie! Wait until I tell you about my hair!"

"Annie Pat," said Eddie, "I don't want to talk about your hair again."

"But *I* want to talk about it," said Anna Patricia, "and you can't stop me."

"Okay!" said Eddie. "Talk to yourself." And he walked away.

Just then Carol ran up to him and said, "Oh, Eddie! Wait until I tell you about poor Gloria's hair."

Eddie couldn't get away. Carol had him backed up against the wall of the school. Eddie let out a deep sigh. "Maybe it would have been better if I had listened to Annie Pat," he said.

CHAPTER 2

THE CHILDREN'S THEATER

THE very last day of school Eddie arrived with the corners of his mouth turned down and his lower lip sticking out. He looked very unhappy. When Anna Patricia saw him, she said, "Hi, Eddie!"

"Hi!" said Eddie, as he threw himself into his seat and put his head in his hands.

"Don't you feel good?" Anna Patricia asked.

"I feel all right," said Eddie.

"Well, what's the matter with you?" said Anna Patricia.

"Nothing," he replied.

"Oh, that's good," said Anna Patricia. "I'm happy too. I'm happy 'cause I'm going to be an actress."

"Leave me alone," said Eddie. "I don't feel good."

"You just said you felt all right," said Anna Patricia.

"Now I don't," said Eddie.

"Have you got a toothache?" Anna Patricia asked.

"No," said Eddie.

"Headache?" said Anna Patricia.

"No," said Eddie.

"Stomach-ache?" said Anna Patricia.

"No," said Eddie.

Carol, who was standing nearby, pricked up her ears and said, "Are you and Eddie playing a guessing game? Can I play?"

"Oh, go drown yourselves!" said Eddie.

"Eddie Wilson!" exclaimed Anna Patricia. "Here I am trying to help you, and you say, 'Go drown yourself.' I guess you'll be sorry you ever talked to me that way when I'm a real live actress."

Eddie went right on holding his head. Anna Patricia looked at him. Then she said, "Eddie, are you mad at me?"

"No!" said Eddie. "I'm not mad at you. I'm just mad."

"What are you mad about?" said Anna Patricia.

"I'm mad because I can't go to Texas and be a cowboy on my Uncle Ed's ranch," replied Eddie.

"You can't?" said Anna Patricia. "How come?"

"Uncle Ed and Aunt Minnie have to go off on some trip," said Eddie.

"Oh, Eddie! That's too bad. Maybe you could go with us and be an actress," said Anna Patricia.

"What!" Eddie cried, taking his head out of his hands at last.

"I mean an actor," said Anna Patricia.

"I don't want to be an actor," said Eddie. "I want to be a cowboy."

"Well," said Anna Patricia, "there are lots of actors on television that are cowboys. Lots!"

That was the last thing that Anna Patricia said to Eddie, because the bell rang for school to begin. When Anna Patricia got home after school, she said to her mother, "Mother, poor Eddie Wilson can't go to Texas and be a cowboy, because his aunt and uncle are going away."

"That's too bad," said her mother. "Is he very disappointed?"

"He feels awful," said Anna Patricia. "I've been thinking. Could he maybe go away with us?"

"Perhaps he could," said her mother. "Of course, there will be your little cousin Davey."

39

"Davey could sleep in my room," said Anna Patricia.

"Oh, I guess we could manage," said Mrs. Wallace. "Shall I ask his mother if he can go?"

"Yes, ask her," said Anna Patricia.

Mrs. Wallace dialed the Wilson's telephone number. When Mrs. Wilson answered, she said, "This is Mary Wallace. Anna Patricia tells me that Eddie can't go to Texas."

"That's right," said Eddie's mother. "He feels very bad about it, but I've been telling him that something else may come along."

Mrs. Wallace laughed. "Perhaps it has come along," she said. "Anna Patricia and I were wondering whether Eddie would like to spend the summer with us. It isn't like a Texas ranch, but the house is right on the water, and we're getting a sailboat. Then, of course, there is the Children's Theater."

"It sounds wonderful!" said Mrs. Wilson. "How kind of you to invite him. I'll tell Eddie about it."

"We should love to have him," said Mrs. Wallace, before she hung up the receiver.

It wasn't long before Eddie dialed Anna Patricia's telephone number. Anna Patricia answered the ring. "Say, Annie Pat," said Eddie, "it's swell of you to want me to spend the summer with you!"

"Are you coming?" Anna Patricia asked.

"Sure!" said Eddie. "It sounds real keen."

"Mother!" Anna Patricia called out. "Eddie's going with us."

By the first of July, Anna Patricia and her mother, Davey, and Eddie were settled in the house by the water. The front of the house faced the road, but the back porch looked out over the water. At high tide it seemed very near. At first it sounded strange to Anna Patricia to hear the water lapping outside the window of her bedroom, but it wasn't long before she became used to it. Then she didn't notice the sound at all.

Eddie couldn't wait for the sailboat to arrive, and

Anna Patricia couldn't wait to see the theater where she was to be an actress.

Eddie was going to have to wait until Saturday, when Anna Patricia's father was arriving for the week end. Anna Patricia's father was a dentist, and he could only come for the week ends. The very next morning after they arrived, Mrs. Wallace drove the three children over to the theater.

"Annie Pat," said Eddie, when they were seated in the car, "this theater business is your business, but it isn't mine. I'm not going to act."

"Nobody has asked you to act, Eddie," said Anna Patricia.

"Well, they might," said Eddie, "and I haven't time, 'cause I'll be busy with the sailboat as soon as I learn how to sail it."

"Can I go in the boat with you, Eddie?" said Davey.

"You're too little. You might fall overboard."

Davey turned to Anna Patricia. "I was a Wise Man

42

in a play once in kindergarten," he said. "Can I be a Wise Man in a play, Anna Patricia?"

"Wise Men are only at Christmas," said Anna Patricia.

"I was a rabbit, too, once," said Davey.

"Rabbits are only at Easter," said Anna Patricia.

"Well, what *can* I do?"

Before anyone could answer Davey's question, Mrs. Wallace stopped the car beside a large wooden building, and they all got out.

"Is this it?" said Eddie. "This doesn't look like a theater. It's right on the wharf."

"Years ago they built whaling boats in it," said Mrs. Wallace, "but it has been made into a theater."

The children ran to the front door, but Anna Patricia's mother called out, "The front door is locked. Mrs. Wells said we would have to use the back door."

"Oh, yes," said Anna Patricia, "the stage door! Oh, it is so exciting to be an actress!"

43

"You're not an actress yet," said Eddie.

Around on the side of the building, near the back, they found a door. Eddie turned the doorknob and pushed against the door. As it opened, Mrs. Wallace said, "I'll go do some marketing. I'll come back for you in about an hour."

The sunshine out of doors was so bright that the inside of the building looked very dark. The children could not see very much when they came through the door. But as their eyes became accustomed to less light, they could see that they had come into a very large room filled with rows of benches. It was as large as the assembly room in the children's school.

To the right of the door, there was a stage that filled the back end of the building.

The children could hear a voice on the stage.

"Oh," whispered Anna Patricia, "it's a rehearsal!"

Then a very loud voice said, "Oh, pickles! I love pickles!"

"Let's sit down here and watch it," said Anna Patricia, pushing Davey down into a seat in the front row.

The children looked up at the stage from the front row. There were about ten children sitting on stools. Each one held a paper plate. A boy about Eddie's age was passing a plate of sandwiches.

"What kind of sandwiches are these?" asked a little girl.

"Chicken," replied the boy.

"They sure look good," Eddie whispered to Anna Patricia. "They look real."

"They wouldn't have real chicken sandwiches for a rehearsal," said Anna Patricia.

"Maybe they don't eat them," said Eddie.

"I guess not," said Anna Patricia. "Just make believe."

"They've got a lot of stuff up there," said Eddie. "Look at that chocolate cake."

"Looks yummy!" said Anna Patricia.

"When do you suppose they eat all that food?" said Eddie.

"I guess after the play is all over."

"Must be pretty stale!" said Eddie.

Just then Mrs. Wells came in the door. She had a parcel in her arm. "Now," she said, "here is the ice cream, and I don't want it to melt."

"Some play!" said Eddie. "They can't keep ice cream. They're going to eat it, sure enough!"

At that moment Mrs. Wells spied the children in the front row. "Why, Anna Patricia," she called, "I didn't see you there! It's so dark when one comes in out of the sunshine." Mrs. Wells came over to the children and said, "Hello, Davey! How are you?"

"Fine!" said Davey. "I was a Wise Man once and I was a rabbit."

"Mrs. Wells," said Anna Patricia, "this is Eddie Wilson. He is staying with us this summer."

Mrs. Wells shook hands with Eddie and said, "How nice. I'm glad to see you, Eddie."

Eddie said, "Thanks. I'm glad to meet you."

"Well, isn't this fun!" said Mrs. Wells. "You just came in time. Come right up on the stage."

"Oh, I'm sorry," said Eddie, "but I don't want to act. I really haven't time. I'm going to be awfully busy with the sailboat."

"What is the name of this play that they are rehearsing?" Anna Patricia asked.

Mrs. Wells laughed. "This isn't a rehearsal," she said. "This is a picnic lunch. We made so much money at our performance last night that the children are having a feast today. You're just in time."

"Oh!" said Eddie. "Well, that's super!"

Mrs. Wells led the three children through the door that led to the stage. On the stage, she introduced all of the children. "We do this after every play," she said.

"Yes," said a boy named Bruce, "we usually have a

supper after the last performance of each play. We call it a Strike Supper."

"Why do you call it a Strike Supper?" Eddie asked.

"'Cause we have to strike down all of the scenery after the last performance," said Bruce.

"Know what, Annie Pat?" said Eddie, sinking his teeth into a chicken sandwich.

"What?" said Anna Patricia, while Eddie chewed a mouthful.

Eddie swallowed and said, "I've changed my mind. I guess I'll be an actor after all."

"An actor!" exclaimed Bruce. "You have to do all kinds of things beside acting. You have to paint scenery and work lights and take care of property and sweep the floor and sell tickets and everything."

"That's O.K." said Eddie. "This food is swell!"

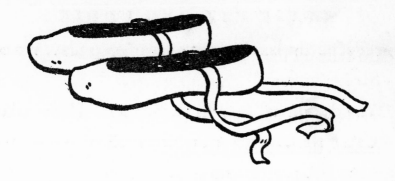

CHAPTER 3

LUMPS IN HER SLIPPERS

THE following morning Anna Patricia and Eddie walked to the theater. It took them a long time, because there was so much to look at. The little harbor was full of sailboats. Eddie tried to count them, but there were so many he lost count. They were all at anchor with their sails down. They bobbed up and down on the blue water and sparkled in the early morning sunshine.

Anna Patricia called out the names that she could read on the boats, *"Ida, Celeste, Patsy, Sistie, Lorna, Pink Lady, Susan."*

"Do they all have girl's names?" Eddie asked.

"Boats are always a she," said Anna Patricia. "Everybody knows that."

"What's the name of the boat your father's bringing up?" said Eddie.

"It doesn't have one yet," said Anna Patricia. "But I guess it will be named after me."

"Is that so!" said Eddie. "Well, there wouldn't be enough room on the end of the boat to put such a name as Anna Patricia. If it was my boat, I'd call it the *Doodlebug*."

"It would have to be *Ladybug*," said Anna Patricia. "I told you, a boat has to be a lady."

"O.K.," said Eddie. "*Ladybug* is a good name. We'll christen it the *Ladybug* when it comes."

While the children were talking, they were walking along the road toward the theater. They stopped from time to time to watch a boy on one of the sailboats, but finally they reached the stage door.

Eddie pushed the door open, and the two children went into the cool gloom of the theater. They could hear a lot of noise before they could see very much. There was a din of banging and thumping, and, over all, the sound of children's voices.

Mrs. Wells was standing in the center of the theater, talking to a girl who was about Anna Patricia's age. Another girl was walking up and down the center aisle with a paper in one hand, while she gestured with the other. She seemed to be talking out loud to herself. Anna Patricia could see another girl behind the back row of benches. She kept kicking her foot in the air and bringing it down on top of the back of the bench.

Eddie walked to the edge of the stage and called up to the boys, "Hey! What are you making up there?"

One of the boys stopped hammering and called back, "We're making the new sets for the next play."

"What's the name of the next play?" Eddie asked.

" 'Cinderella'!" replied a boy with a paintbrush in his hand.

" 'Cinderella'!" Eddie repeated. " 'Cinderella'!" He ran over to Anna Patricia, who was standing nearby. "Listen, Annie Pat," he said. "You don't think they'll want me to be the Prince in 'Cinderella,' do you? Because I'm not going to do it."

"Oh, of course not!" said Anna Patricia.

"I'm no glass slipper tryer-on-er," said Eddie.

"They'd never choose *you* for the Prince," said Anna Patricia.

"Is that so?" said Eddie. "I'd like to know why not?"

"Because you don't *look* like a prince," said Anna Patricia.

"I don't, don't I!" exclaimed Eddie. "Well, what do I look like?"

Anna Patricia looked at Eddie very hard. Finally she said, "Maybe a little like one of the white mice."

56

Before Eddie could reply, Mrs. Wells had spotted the two children. She called to them, "Come here, Anna Patricia and Eddie."

They went over to Mrs. Wells, and she introduced them to the girl beside her. Her name was Liza. "Liza is going to be Cinderella," she said. "Liza was with us last summer."

Then Mrs. Wells called to the girl who seemed to be talking to herself. "Christie," she said, "this is Anna Patricia, and this is Eddie."

"Hello!" Christie called back. "I'm memorizing my lines. I'm the stepmother."

"Hello!" replied Eddie and Anna Patricia together.

Mrs. Wells waved her arm toward the back of the room and said, "That's Debbie back there. She's going to be the fairy godmother."

When Debbie heard her name, she looked across the room and called out, "Hi!"

"Hi!" said Eddie.

"Hello!" said Anna Patricia. "What's Debbie doing?" Anna Patricia asked Mrs. Wells.

"She does ballet," said Mrs. Wells. "She's practicing."

"Oh!" said Anna Patricia. She didn't like to say, "What am I going to be?" so she said, "What's Eddie going to be?"

"Eddie is going to help print the tickets," replied Mrs. Wells.

"Oh, that's great!" exclaimed Eddie. "Do you have a printing press?"

"Yes, we have a little hand press," said Mrs. Wells. "You can help Jim. You'll find him in that little room beside the stage."

Eddie ran off to help Jim print tickets. He was delighted with his job, and he wasn't going to have to be a prince!

"And now, Anna Patricia," said Mrs. Wells, "what would you like to do?"

"Could I be an ugly sister?" said Anna Patricia. "I could make myself look real ugly."

"I think you had better start in the theater with a smaller part," said Mrs. Wells. "Can you dance? There's a fairy ballet in the play."

"Oh, I go to dancing school," said Anna Patricia. "We always wear white gloves."

"Never mind the gloves," said Mrs. Wells. "Run back to Debbie and ask her to show you the steps."

Anna Patricia ran to the back of the theater. Debbie was still kicking her foot into the air and bringing it down on top of the back of the bench.

"Debbie," said Anna Patricia, "Mrs. Wells says you are to show me the steps. I know how to dance. I go to dancing school. I wear white gloves and everything."

"In ballet you don't wear white gloves," said Debbie. "You wear toe shoes. Do you have toe shoes?"

"You mean those ballet slippers with lumps in the toes?"

"Well, yes!" said Debbie. "Only I don't think it sounds very nice to call them lumps."

"But that's what they are!" said Anna Patricia. "If you don't have lumps, you can't stand up in them."

"Oh, real ballet dancers do it right on their toes," said Debbie.

"Don't you have any lumps in yours?" said Anna Patricia.

"Well, I don't call them lumps," said Debbie. Then, changing the subject, she said, "You'd better begin by limbering up. Kick your leg as high as you can and put your foot on top of the back of this bench."

Anna Patricia kicked her leg in the air and brought her foot down on top of the bench with such a bang that she lost her balance and fell on the floor. The bench toppled over on top of her. In the empty room it made a horrible racket. It brought everyone running, even Eddie and Jim.

Mrs. Wells and Eddie lifted the bench, and Debbie

helped Anna Patricia to her feet. "Are you hurt?" Debbie asked.

"My head!" said Anna Patricia. "That bench hit me right on my forehead." There were tears in Anna Patricia's eyes. She tried to rub them away.

"You shouldn't kick so hard," said Debbie. "You kicked as though you were kicking a football. Remember, you're a dancer."

"I'll try it again tomorrow," said Anna Patricia, rubbing her head.

"Perhaps Eddie had better walk home with you," said Mrs. Wells, putting her arm around Anna Patricia.

"Sure!" said Eddie. "Come along, Annie Pat."

Everyone went to the door with Anna Patricia. She felt very important. Outside the door, in the bright sunshine, they all waved good-by to Anna Patricia and Eddie. There were Mrs. Wells and all of the boys. There were Debbie and Christie and Liza.

Suddenly, in the sunshine, the girls looked different. Anna Patricia stood still and said, "Oh, Eddie! Look! Debbie and Liza and Christie all have red hair."

"Actresses!" said Eddie. "Why don't you stop trying to be one and help print tickets?"

"No!" said Anna Patricia. "I've decided to be a ballet dancer."

"You'd better wet your handkerchief and bathe that bump on your head," said Eddie.

"Let's go out on that wharf," said Anna Patricia. "I can dip my handkerchief into the water."

"O.K.," said Eddie, "but don't fall in."

"I won't fall in," said Anna Patricia.

The children went out on the dock, and Anna Patricia dipped her handkerchief into the water. She held it to her forehead and looked at the water. After a moment she said, "Oh, look, Eddie! Look at that big cork, floating in the water. Can you get it?"

"What do you want with it?" Eddie asked. "It's one of those big corks from a fishing net."

"Well, I want it!" said Anna Patricia. "It will be just the thing to make those lumps to go inside my bedroom slippers."

"Lumps in your bedroom slippers!" exclaimed Eddie. "Who wants lumps in their bedroom slippers!"

"Eddie," said Anna Patricia, "I can't get any ballet slippers for days and days away up here. I have to practice in my bedroom slippers."

"Annie Pat, that cork is twice as big as your bedroom slippers," said Eddie.

"I know that, Eddie! But you can cut it into two pieces and make them just the right size. Now hurry up. You can reach it now. I'll hold your feet, so you won't fall in."

Eddie lay down on the dock and reached out. The cork floated nearer and nearer. Anna Patricia held on to Eddie's legs. She also held her breath. At last

Eddie could touch it with one finger. Then he had it in his hand.

"Now," said Anna Patricia, "let's take it home, and after lunch you can cut it. That will be fun, won't it?"

"Oh, sure!" said Eddie. "It's always fun to carve something, and this cork will be good for that."

After lunch Eddie cut up the cork into round pieces to go into Anna Patricia's pale pink bedroom slippers. He cut and pared and scraped while Anna Patricia watched. Then he pushed them into the toes of the slippers. Then he pulled them out. He cut and he pared some more. At last they fitted into the toes of Anna Patricia's bedroom slippers.

"There!" said Eddie. "That's the best I can do."

"Oh, that's wonderful!" exclaimed Anna Patricia. "I can't wait to try them on."

Anna Patricia poked her toes into one of the slippers. She got her toes in, but when she tried to pull the slipper on, her heel wouldn't go in. "Oh, dear!" she

said. "Now I can't put my slippers on. They're too little!" She sat looking at her slippers with a wrinkled forehead. Soon her face brightened. "I know!" she said. "I'll use Mother's bedroom slippers."

Anna Patricia ran upstairs to her mother's bedroom and came back with her mother's blue slippers. She took the corks out of her slippers and put them into her mother's. She pushed her toes into the slippers and pulled on the heels, but when she stood on her toes, the heels fell off.

Eddie looked at Anna Patricia. Then he began to laugh. He laughed and laughed.

"What are you laughing at, Eddie?" said Anna Patricia.

"I just thought!" said Eddie. "You could be both of Cinderella's ugly sisters. Do you remember? One sister's feet were too big for the glass slippers, and the other sister's feet were too little."

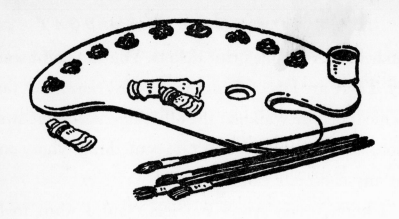

CHAPTER 4

HOW TO FEEL LIKE A BOAT

THE next morning Anna Patricia set out with Eddie for the theater.

"I don't feel much like going to the theater," said Anna Patricia. "I don't have any ballet slippers, so I can't be in the fairy ballet, and I can't have a part in the play. So what *can* I do?"

"There are lots of things to do," said Eddie. "You

can help Jim and me print tickets. You can paint scenery. There are lots of things to do. Just remember that picnic lunch they all had the other day with that swell chocolate cake. If you don't do something, you won't get any chocolate cake."

"I know," said Anna Patricia, "but I want to *be* something."

Anna Patricia and Eddie had turned into the lane that led to the theater, and there, in the middle of the lane, sat a lady on a folding stool. In front of her was an easel, and on the easel was a white board. Dabs of bright colors showed here and there on the white board. The lady was wearing a broad-brimmed hat and a smock that looked like a patchwork quilt.

"There's an artist," said Eddie.

"Oh, yes!" said Anna Patricia. "She's painting a picture."

Eddie and Anna Patricia quickened their footsteps. Soon they were standing behind the artist. They watched her as she put paint on the board with a long-handled brush.

"What is she painting?" Anna Patricia whispered to Eddie.

"I don't know," said Eddie. "I guess maybe she's just painting."

"She has to be painting something," said Anna Patricia. "If she was just painting, she wouldn't be sitting in the middle of this road."

Eddie and Anna Patricia looked around. There were two little houses. There were some trees. There was a dock and some water. There were sailboats. Then they came closer to the painting and took a good look. There were no houses in the painting. There were no trees, no docks, no water, no boats.

The children moved still closer. Now they were standing one on each side of the artist. The artist had stopped painting. She was holding her brush in her left hand. With her right hand, she was squeezing a little mound of white paint onto a white tray that lay across her knees.

"That looks just like toothpaste," said Anna Patricia.

The artist jumped with surprise. "Yes, it does," she said, "but it's paint." Then she lifted the lid of a box that was lying on the ground. "See?" she said. "These are my tubes of paint."

"Oh!" said Anna Patricia. "My paints are in little pans."

"Sometimes paints come in jars," said Eddie.

"Oh, yes," said the artist, "but they are water colors. These are oil paints."

"My mother buys mustard in tubes like these," said Anna Patricia, "and catchup and strawberry jam and orange marmalade and apricot, too."

"I have red-and-white toothpaste in a tube," said Eddie. "I'll bet you don't have any red-and-white paint in a tube."

"I have green," said Anna Patricia.

Eddie moved up closer to the painting. He peered at it. Then he looked around. He looked back at the painting. Then he said, "What are you painting?"

The artist waved her paintbrush. "I'm painting that boat," she said.

Eddie and Anna Patricia looked at the boat. Then they looked at the painting. It didn't look like a boat to Eddie or to Anna Patricia.

"It doesn't *look* like a boat," said Eddie.

"Oh, my dear boy!" replied the artist. "It isn't supposed to *look* like a boat. It's supposed to make you *feel* like a boat."

Eddie opened his eyes very wide and said, "You mean me?"

"Of course!" replied the artist. Then she spread her arms wide and waved her paintbrush. "Everyone who looks at this painting will feel like a boat."

"Oh, I think that's wonderful!" said Anna Patricia. "I'm going to stand right here until I feel like a boat."

"Well, I have to go print tickets," said Eddie. "So long!"

"Good-by!" said Anna Patricia.

"Good-by, little boy!" said the artist.

"I wish I had something to sit on," said Anna Patricia, "while I'm waiting to feel like a boat."

"Sit down on my paintbox," said the artist.

Anna Patricia squatted down on the paintbox with her legs crossed under her. She watched as the paint went on in thick lumps. "It's nice and gooey, isn't it?" said Anna Patricia.

"Yes," said the artist. "I always use plenty of paint. I always say, 'Don't be stingy.'"

Just then Anna Patricia noticed a paper bag on the ground beside the easel. She could see a banana inside the bag. It looked like a nice ripe banana.

"I don't feel like a boat yet," said Anna Patricia, "but I guess if I stay here I will. I'm just crazy to feel like a boat. I never felt like one before."

"Oh," said the artist, "you will, my child, you will! I can tell that you are a real artist, like me."

"Oh, I'd like to be a real artist," said Anna Patricia.

"You can be," said the artist. "Just don't be afraid to use plenty of paint. Don't be stingy."

Anna Patricia looked at the banana and said, "Maybe if I weren't so hungry, I would feel like a boat."

"Would you like to have a banana?" the artist asked.

"A banana would be nice," said Anna Patricia.

The artist put down her brush and reached for the paper bag. She pulled out the banana and handed it to Anna Patricia.

"Oh, thank you!" said Anna Patricia.

Anna Patricia pulled down the skin of the banana and took a large bite. Then she said, "I ate a banana

once when I was on a boat, and I was awful seasick. You don't think I'll be seasick when I feel like a boat, do you?"

"No, no, my child!" said the artist. "Eat the banana."

Anna Patricia ate the banana. When she finished it, she said to the artist, "Do you feel like a boat?"

"Yes, indeed!" the artist replied. "I feel like a little sailboat, skimming across the blue, blue water. You must be an artist, little girl. When you are an artist, you feel."

"If I painted a dragon, would I feel like a dragon?" said Anna Patricia.

"Of course!" replied the artist.

"I can't wait to begin to be an artist," said Anna Patricia.

"You must begin at once," said the artist. "Here! You can have this board for your first painting."

"Oh, thank you!" said Anna Patricia, tucking the white board under her arm.

77

Then Anna Patricia stared very, very hard at the painting on the easel. She couldn't make herself feel like a boat. She thought perhaps if she held her breath she could feel like a boat, so she held her breath. She held it until she began to feel very lightheaded.

Suddenly she let out her breath and cried, "Oh! I feel like a boat! I feel like a boat!"

"Oh! I knew you would!" cried the artist. "I knew you would! You are an artist, just like me."

"Good-by!" shouted Anna Patricia. "I can't wait to paint a dragon."

Anna Patricia ran all the way home. She couldn't wait to start painting. It wasn't until she reached home that she thought of paints. After all, she couldn't paint without paints.

Anna Patricia stood in the middle of the kitchen with the clean white board hanging from her hand. She had a box of water colors and a brush, but Anna

Patricia didn't want to paint with water colors. She wanted something thick and gooey.

Suddenly she had an idea. She went to the pantry closet and opened the door. There on the shelf were some tubes.

A half hour later her little cousin Davey came in from the beach. "What are you doing, Anna Patricia?" Davey asked.

"I'm painting," said Anna Patricia.

Davey stood beside Anna Patricia and looked at the painting that she had propped against the back of a chair. Then he looked at a white platter on which there were little mushy piles, all different in color. There were white, and red-and-white mixed. There were light green and red and orange and yellow and dark red and yellowish brown.

Davey turned from the platter to the painting. Pointing to the painting, he said, "What's that?"

"It's a dragon," said Anna Patricia.

"It doesn't look like a dragon," said Davey. "All that red stuff looks like strawberry jam. It doesn't look like a dragon at all."

"It isn't supposed to *look* like a dragon," said Anna Patricia. "It's supposed to make you *feel* like a dragon."

"It doesn't make me feel like a dragon," said Davey. "It makes me feel like eating strawberry jam." Davey stuck his finger into the pile of red into which Anna Patricia was putting her paintbrush.

"Davey!" cried Anna Patricia. "Keep your fingers out of my paint." But Davey had already stuck his finger into his mouth.

"It *is* strawberry jam!" cried Davey.

Just then Eddie came in. "Eddie," cried Davey, "Anna Patricia is painting with strawberry jam!"

Eddie looked at the painting and at the messy platter. "Annie Pat!" he cried. "What are you doing?"

"I wanted to paint a dragon," said Anna Patricia, "and I didn't have any of that nice gooey paint. But this make-believe paint is fine, if you put it on thick."

Eddie looked at the platter of make-believe paint. He pointed to each one and called out, "Strawberry jam! Apricot jam! Orange marmalade! Mustard! Catchup! Green toothpaste! White toothpaste! And of all the nerve! My red-and-white stripe toothpaste! Of all the nerve!"

"I thought it would make pink!" said Anna Patricia. "But it isn't very pink."

"Annie Pat," said Eddie, "you're making an awful mess!"

"Eddie, you're not an artist, but I am," said Anna Patricia. "I can feel like a boat, and I can feel like a dragon."

"Well, I feel hungry!" said Eddie.

"So do I!" said Davey. "I want some bread and strawberry jam."

"Anyway," said Anna Patricia, "I've decided what I'm going to be. I'm going to be an artist."

"You'd better clean up that awful mess of jam and mustard and toothpaste," said Eddie, "before your mother sees it. It makes me sick to look at it."

"I think the painting is beautiful," said Anna Patricia, "but I guess I'd better wash this platter. After all, I didn't use very much jam or mustard or toothpaste."

"What are you going to do with the painting?" Eddie asked. "It's so sticky you could use it for flypaper, to catch flies."

"Eddie Wilson," exclaimed Anna Patricia, "you just do not know anything about art! I have a nice frame with a glass in it, and I'm going to frame this painting."

"You'd better frame it quick, Annie Pat," said Eddie, "before it starts catching flies."

Just then Anna Patricia's mother came in.

"Oh, Aunt Mary!" cried Davey. "Anna Patricia just made a flycatcher."

"It is *not* a flycatcher!" said Anna Patricia. "It's a painting. Look, Mother! How does it make you feel?"

Mrs. Wallace leaned over and looked at the painting. When she straightened up, she looked at Anna Patricia and said, "It makes me feel that you have been a naughty girl."

"Oh, but Mother!" exclaimed Anna Patricia. "Don't you feel at all like a dragon?"

"Yes, I do," replied her mother. "I feel like a mad dragon, and you shall have no bread and jam for a whole week."

"And no mustard and no catchup?" asked Davey. "And no toothpaste?"

"Well, yes," said Anna Patricia's mother, "a little toothpaste."

"Oh, dear!" sighed Anna Patricia. "It's hard to be an artist. Nobody understands me!"

CHAPTER 5

THE *LADYBUG* ARRIVES

THE evening Anna Patricia's father brought the sailboat down from the city there was a great deal of excitement. He brought it on a little trailer, hitched to the back of his car. The mast, which was lying in the boat, stuck out so far that he had a red flag flying from the end of it. Beside the mast was the boom. The sail was in a bag in the cockpit.

Anna Patricia, Eddie, and Davey were out front when the car and the boat arrived. "Oh, here's the sailboat!" Eddie cried. "Here's the sailboat! Here's the *Ladybug!*"

The three children rushed up to the trailer to look at the sailboat.

"What kind of sailboat is it?" Eddie asked. "Is it a Moth?"

"No," replied Anna Patricia's father, "it's a sneakbox."

Davey rushed into the house calling out, "Aunt Mary! Uncle Ray has brought a thiefbox."

"A thiefbox!" exclaimed Mrs. Wallace. "What's a thiefbox?"

"It's a boat," said Davey.

Mrs. Wallace came outside to look at the boat.

"See!" said Davey. "There's the thiefbox."

"No, Davey," said Eddie. "Not a thiefbox. A sneakbox."

"Oh!" said Davey. "You mean it's sneaky? Why is it sneaky?"

"Yes, Daddy," said Anna Patricia, "tell us why it's called a sneakbox. That's a funny name for a sailboat."

Anna Patricia's father leaned against the boat and said, "This is the kind of boat that's used for duck hunting. The hunters can sneak up on the ducks with it. They can shoot the ducks before the ducks can hear the boat coming. Somebody had a good idea when he decided to fit a sneakbox with a sail. It makes a fine sailboat."

"Are we going to sneak up on ducks?" Davey asked.

"Silly!" exclaimed Anna Patricia. "There aren't any ducks here."

"There are sea gulls," said Davey.

"Sea gulls are different," said Eddie. "You don't shoot sea gulls."

"Now," said Anna Patricia's father, "the question

is, who is going to help me carry this boat down to the dock?"

"I am," said Eddie.

"Eddie," said Dr. Wallace, "you would have to be an elephant. This boat is heavy. It will take four strong men to carry it."

"I can help carry the mast, can't I?" said Eddie.

"You certainly can," said Dr. Wallace, "just as soon as I get it unfastened."

Mrs. Wallace and the children watched while Anna Patricia's father unfastened the mast. They watched him take the boom out. Then he and Eddie carried them to the dock and laid them down. They went back to the boat for the sail and carried it to the dock.

When they returned to the boat, Dr. Wallace said, "Now three strong men are all we need."

"Maybe Mr. Brown, who lives next door, would help," Anna Patricia suggested.

"I'm sure he would, but he's gone off for the day, fishing," said her mother.

"What about asking Mr. Upson, across the road? He'd help," said Eddie.

"He has gone fishing with Mr. Brown," said Mrs. Wallace.

"Oh, dear!" sighed Anna Patricia. "I thought we could go sailing before supper."

"We can't go sailing," said her father, "until I learn how to sail this boat."

Anna Patricia, Eddie, and Davey all looked at Dr. Wallace in surprise. Anna Patricia's mouth was wide open. When she closed it, she said, "Daddy, don't you know how to sail the boat?"

"No, I don't," her father replied.

"But, Daddy!" exclaimed Anna Patricia. "I thought you knew how to do *everything*."

"Well, that's very nice of you, Anna Patricia," said her father, "but I don't know how to sail a boat."

"What's the use of putting the boat in the water, if you can't sail it?" Anna Patricia asked.

"I hope to learn very soon," her father replied.

"Is it easy to learn?" Eddie asked.

"I believe so," said Dr. Wallace. "If I can ever get the boat into the water, I think I can learn to sail it."

Just then, the bakery truck came around the corner. "Oh, here's the breadman!" said Anna Patricia. "Maybe he'll help you."

"But we need three breadmen," said her father.

"Oh, dear!" said Anna Patricia.

"Maybe if we telephoned the police, they'd send three policemen around to help," said Eddie.

"They only have two policemen on the whole police force," said Dr. Wallace.

"Well, what about the fire department?" said Eddie. "Firemen are always strong."

"They don't have a fire department here," said Dr. Wallace. "When there's a fire, they blow a whistle, and everybody runs to put the fire out. It's what is called a volunteer fire department."

"Here comes the milkman!" Davey called out, pointing down the road.

"Maybe he has a helper with him," said Eddie.

"He wouldn't have two helpers," said Anna Patricia.

"I guess not," said Eddie.

The milkman came and went. As he went, he said, "Nice boat you got there."

"Thanks," said Anna Patricia's father. Then he mopped his forehead and said, "I'm thirsty."

"Let's go inside and have some lemonade," said Mrs. Wallace. "I have a pitcherful in the refrigerator."

Dr. and Mrs. Wallace and the three children went indoors. Mrs. Wallace took the pitcher of lemonade out of the refrigerator and poured out five glasses. Davey gulped his right down and ran back to the boat. The rest sat down on the porch and drank their lemonade more slowly.

"When will we have the name *Ladybug* painted on the end of the boat?" Anna Patricia asked.

"You mustn't call it the end of the boat," said her father. "You must call it the stern."

"Well, when will we have the name painted on the stern?" said Anna Patricia.

"Just as soon as we can get the painter to do it," replied her father.

Suddenly Davey rushed into the house yelling, "Come quick! Come quick!"

Everyone jumped up. "What is it?" said Anna Patricia's father.

"Come quick!" cried Davey. "There are three sailors! Three sailors, coming up the road."

Everyone ran out front and, sure enough, there were three sailors looking at the sailboat. One was tall, one was short, and one was fat.

When they saw the children and Anna Patricia's mother and father, they said, "Hi!"

93

They were answered with a chorus of hi's.

"Nice boat," said the tall sailor.

"We want to put it in the water," said Davey.

"Sure!" said the short sailor. "Not much good out of water."

"I wonder if you fellows would be kind enough to help me carry it down to the dock?" asked Dr. Wallace.

"Sure we would," said the sailors all together.

"We certainly would appreciate it," said Anna Patricia's father. Then he added, "I'm Dr. Wallace."

The sailor who had spoken first shook hands with Dr. Wallace and said, "I'm Artie." Then, turning to the short sailor, he said, "This is Steve," and, waving his hand toward the fat sailor, he said, "This is Mike."

Dr. Wallace shook hands with Steve and Mike and introduced everyone else.

In a few minutes, the three sailors and Dr. Wallace had the boat on their shoulders and, with the three chil-

dren and Mrs. Wallace in the rear, they paraded to the dock.

"Want us to rig her up for you?" Steve asked.

"That would be very kind," said Dr. Wallace.

The sailors set to work, while everyone stood by watching. It wasn't long before the mast was in place, the boom was fastened, and the sail was up. When they had finished, Artie said, "Now, who is the sailor in the family?"

Anna Patricia's father and mother laughed. "Nobody, yet," said Dr. Wallace.

Artie looked at Eddie and said, "You look as if you have the makings of a good sailor."

"Me?" said Eddie, and he grinned from ear to ear.

"What about me?" said Anna Patricia.

"You'll make a good crew," said Mike.

"What about me?" said Davey.

"You'll make a good passenger, if you'll sit still," said Artie.

Artie put his hand on Eddie's shoulder and said, "Suppose I take out the captain here, and teach him the ropes?"

"Fine!" said Dr. Wallace. "Go ahead."

"Can we go too?" said Anna Patricia.

"I think I'd better take Eddie alone," said Artie. "You wait here with Steve and Mike. When I come back, I'll take you and the little fellow."

"All right," said Anna Patricia, "but don't be long."

While Steve and Mike held the boat, Artie and Eddie stepped in.

Suddenly Anna Patricia cried out, "Oh, wait a minute! Wait!"

She ran into the house and came back with the lemonade pitcher. There was just a little bit of lemonade left in the pitcher. Anna Patricia ran all the way out on the dock with it. Everyone wondered what she was going to do.

"I have to christen the boat before she sails," Anna

Patricia cried. She lifted the pitcher above the sail-boat and poured the lemonade over the stern. As she did so, she called out, "I christen you the *Ladybug*."

"You christened the wrong end," said Artie. "You always christen the bow."

"Oh, dear!" said Anna Patricia. "Does it make any difference? I can make some more lemonade."

"It will probably sail backwards all the time," said Steve.

Everyone laughed. Even Anna Patricia knew that Steve was only fooling.

"It won't sail backwards with Artie at the helm," said Mike. "He grew up in a sailboat."

The group on the dock watched as the sailboat, with Artie and Eddie in it, glided away. They watched it grow smaller and smaller. When it was lost among all of the other sailboats in the bay, Anna Patricia said, "No one out there will know that it's the *Ladybug*."

"But we know it," said Davey.

Mrs. Wallace picked up the pitcher and said, "I'll make some more lemonade. Let's sit on the lawn until they come back."

When Eddie and Artie returned, everyone ran back to the dock. Steve helped Eddie out of the sailboat and said, "How did it go?"

"Oh, it's great!" said Eddie.

"Eddie is a real salt!" said Artie.

Eddie looked very pleased.

Artie turned to Anna Patricia and Davey and said, "Now I'll take the crew and the passenger."

"I don't want to be just a passenger," said Davey. "Why can't I be a crow, too?"

"Not crow, Davey!" said Anna Patricia. "Crew."

"When you get bigger, you can be crew," said Artie. "Meanwhile, I think you'd better wear a life jacket."

Eddie ran to the house and returned with a bright orange life jacket. He helped Davey into it. "Don't fall overboard, Davey, just because you have it on," said Eddie, as Davey was helped into the boat.

"I won't fall overboard," said Davey.

Once again everybody waved as the sailboat took off.

"I learned a lot," said Eddie to Dr. Wallace. "I learned to handle the sheet and the centerboard and the tiller. It's wonderful! And just think! I learned from a real sailor!"

Dr. Wallace turned to the other two sailors standing beside him and said, "How long are you boys going to be around here?"

"Our destroyer is out there in the harbor," said Mike. "We have the week end free."

"How about coming back tomorrow and spending the day with us?" Dr. Wallace asked.

"We should love to have you," said Anna Patricia's mother.

"You'll get a swell dinner," said Eddie. "Aunt Mary is a super cook. She can make wonderful pies."

"You don't have to coax us," said Steve. "You know

there's nothing a sailor likes better than messing around with boats."

Everyone laughed.

When the sailboat returned, Anna Patricia said, "It was wonderful, and I've decided something. When I grow up, I'm going to be a lady sailor."

"That's the girl!" said Artie. "Join the Navy and see the world."

"I fell overboard," said Davey. "But I wasn't scared. Artie pulled me in. I'm going to learn to be a crow."

"Crew, Davey!" said Anna Patricia. "Crew!"

CHAPTER 6

THE HOSE COMMITTEE

By the time Anna Patricia's ballet slippers arrived it was too late for her to be in the fairy ballet. She was so disappointed that Mrs. Wells said that she could be a statue in the garden scene.

The garden scene showed the staircase where Cinderella loses her slipper and the Prince finds it. It was also the scene for the fairy ballet. Mrs. Wells was trying to make the scene as beautiful as possible. The lighting was to be like moonlight. The committee on lights had arranged it very carefully.

Anna Patricia was very happy to be in the play, even though she could not dance with the fairies and did not have a speaking part.

"It isn't very important," said Eddie, "but you'll get in on the supper anyway."

"Well," said Anna Patricia, "there are lots of actors and actresses and a lot of dancers, but there's only one statue. That's me!"

"You'll have to stand awfully still," said Eddie. "I don't think you'll be very good at standing still."

"Oh, I am, Eddie!" cried Anna Patricia. "I can stand stiller than anything."

Anna Patricia rushed home to tell her mother all about it. "I'm going to be covered with some white make-up, so that I'll look like white marble, and I'm going to have a white drapery on me and a wreath of white flowers on my head and a bunch of white flowers in my hands. And I'll stand on a pedestal. I stand just like this."

Anna Patricia took the pose and held a make-believe bunch of flowers in her hands. "I look down," she said, "into a bathtub full of water."

This surprised her mother. "Whatever for?" she said. "What's a bathtub full of water doing on the stage?"

"Oh, that's supposed to be a pool. No one will know it's a bathtub, because it has rocks and bushes that hide everything but the water. They hide my pedestal, too. Of course, the water keeps leaking out, because the bathtub has a hole in it, but there's a garden hose that runs water into the tub while it leaks out of the hole."

"Won't the water flood the stage?" asked her mother.

"No," said Anna Patricia. "You see, the hose committee has it all fixed. Jim and Eddie are the hose committee. They have a funnel in under the hole in the tub, with a hose fastened to the funnel. So the funnel takes the water out, and the garden hose puts the water in."

"I see," said her mother. "I hope it works."

"Oh, it works fine," said Eddie, who had just come in. "Jim and I are the hose committee."

"So I hear," said Anna Patricia's mother.

"Jim's wonderful!" said Eddie. "He can do anything. It's all fixed up for the rehearsal tomorrow."

The next day, when Anna Patricia arrived at the theater for the rehearsal, Eddie and Jim were testing the hose. "Everything is O.K.," said Jim.

"Now, Anna Patricia," said Mrs. Wells, "here's a wreath for your head. The bunch of artificial flowers isn't here yet. Just hold this bunch of cosmos. Remember, you have to keep very, very still. Not a move."

"I know," said Anna Patricia, putting the wreath on her head and picking up the bunch of flowers.

"Be careful when you get up on the pedestal," said

Jim, "Step right in the middle of it, and stay in the middle."

"I know!" said Anna Patricia, as she stepped up.

Anna Patricia took her position and looked into the water. All was quiet. The music began for the fairy ballet.

In a moment, five little girls glided out from the wings on each side of the stage. They danced and formed a circle. Then the fairy godmother came on the stage on tiptoe with a wand in her hand. A tiny light, like a firefly, showed on the tip of the wand. She danced a solo while the fairy ballet posed in a circle.

Anna Patricia held her pose perfectly. She was exactly like a statue. You could hardly see her breathe.

But Anna Patricia was not as calm as she looked. She had something on her mind. The water in the bathtub was not acting as it should. Something must be the matter with the hose on the funnel, she thought.

The water was trickling over the rocks that hid the

tub. It was running down around the bushes. It would soon make little streams of water on the stage, and the fairies would slip in it and perhaps fall down.

Anna Patricia wondered where the hose committee was. They were supposed to watch the hoses backstage. She decided to try to call Eddie. She and Eddie had learned how to whistle by putting their upper teeth over their lower lip. They used the whistle to signal each other. Anna Patricia knew that Eddie was not far off behind the scenery. He would know, if she whistled, that something was wrong.

When the first trickle of water appeared on the floor of the stage, Anna Patricia decided that the ballet music was so loud that, if she whistled, Eddie would hear it behind her, but that the music would keep the whistle from being heard out front. So Anna Patricia whistled. She whistled at the very moment that the music stopped being loud and became very soft.

Anna Patricia's whistle sounded through the whole

theater. The ballet stopped. Everyone turned and looked at the garden statue.

"Anna Patricia!" cried Mrs. Wells from the front row. "Whatever made you do that?"

"I was just trying to get the hose committee. Something is the matter. The bathtub is leaking."

Eddie and Jim appeared in the wings.

"What's the matter with the hose committee?" said Mrs. Wells. "Are you asleep?"

"I guess the hose came loose from the funnel," said Jim, dashing out to investigate.

"If you can't keep the hose and the funnel together, we'll have to give up the pool," said Mrs. Wells.

"Oh, it looks so pretty!" said Anna Patricia.

"It'll be O.K.," said Jim, returning. "Eddie and I will watch it better."

"Now, everybody back. Start the music where we left off," said Mrs. Wells.

The water stopped running. The ballet dancers took

up their dance, and all went smoothly to the finish. They danced off the stage and the music stopped.

In a moment, at the top of the stairs, Cinderella appeared in her beautiful white ball gown. The Prince, wearing pale blue velvet, escorted her by the hand. The Prince began to recite his lines.

Anna Patricia couldn't listen because she had another problem. A little bug had flown off the bunch of flowers and had lighted on Anna Patricia's nose. Anna Patricia looked cross-eyed down her nose. She could see the little bug right on the tip of it. It wasn't walking around. It was just sitting there. She wished the bug would get off and fly away.

Anna Patricia tried to wrinkle her nose. It didn't do any good. The bug just sat. She stuck out her lower lip and blew her breath up. The bug sat.

Suddenly the clock struck the hour. Bong! Bong! Bong! Bong! Bong! Bong! Bong! Bong! Bong! Bong! Bong! Bong! It was midnight.

Just as the twelfth stroke died away, the bug on Anna Patricia's nose decided to go for a walk. It walked around the tip of Anna Patricia's nose and tickled it.

As Cinderella fled down the garden stairs, the garden statue sneezed. She sneezed so hard that her wreath of flowers fell off into the tub of water.

Cinderella stopped in her flight.

"Anna Patricia!" Mrs. Wells called out. "What's the matter now?"

"It was a bug," said Anna Patricia. "It was on my nose. I think it was a ladybug."

"Ladybug or not," said Mrs. Wells, "you cannot behave this way at the performance tomorrow night."

"Oh, I won't!" said Anna Patricia. "There won't be any ladybugs, because my flowers will be artificial. And the water wasn't my fault. It was the fault of the hose committee."

"Well," said Mrs. Wells, "I'll just hope for the best."

When the rehearsal was over, Anna Patricia scooped her wreath out of the water and hung it on a peg to dry.

The next evening the theater was filled with children and grownups, who had come to see the first performance of "Cinderella." Anna Patricia was on her pedestal, wearing her wreath, holding her artificial flowers, and looking down into the water. Moonlight flooded the scene. It did indeed look like fairyland.

The opening strains of the ballet music sounded. Anna Patricia felt a thrill go up and down her backbone. It was beautiful, and she hoped she looked beautiful. Everyone had clapped when the curtain had gone up, so she guessed it all looked very pretty.

Just as the ballet was about to come out, the garden hose sprang a little leak, and a spray of water came right up over Anna Patricia. But Anna Patricia didn't budge, and she didn't make a sound. She just stood there in the center of a fountain. When the

audience saw the fountain begin, they clapped louder than before.

The fairy ballet began. The Fairy Godmother danced. When the ballet was over, Cinderella and the Prince appeared. Through the rest of the scene, Anna Patricia took her shower bath. Her curls were soaked. Her drapery was soaked. Her wreath and her bunch of flowers were soaked, but Anna Patricia didn't move.

When the scene was over and the curtain had fallen, Anna Patricia stepped down from her pedestal.

Mrs. Wells rushed up to her and gathered a dripping Anna Patricia into her arms. "You were wonderful, darling!" she said. "That fountain was simply beautiful."

"Well, I'm glad," said Anna Patricia. "The hose committee isn't much good, is it?"

CHAPTER 7

THAT MAN WITH A BEARD

Aɴɴᴀ Patricia liked doing so many things that it was hard for her to decide each morning what she wanted to do.

Eddie did not have such a hard time making up his mind. He loved the sailboat. Anna Patricia loved the sailboat too, and she and Eddie spent a lot of time on the dock. Artie had showed him how to tie the ropes.

He could even make some of the sailors' knots. Two of Eddie's greatest treasures were an old spyglass and an ancient anchor, which he had bought in a junk shop.

Knots bored Anna Patricia, and she couldn't look through the spyglass all of the time. Instead she was always wandering off to see what was going on in the village.

Not far from the Children's Theater there was an art school. It was for grownups, but Anna Patricia often pushed the door open and looked inside. She liked the way the big room smelled. It smelled of oil paint.

Anna Patricia liked to see what was going on, too. All of the artists stood behind their easels, painting pictures. They were gathered around a platform. Once there was an old fisherman sitting on the platform, and everyone was painting the fisherman. Once there was a beautiful red-haired girl in a green silk dress, and everyone was painting a picture of her.

One day when Anna Patricia stuck her head in the door there wasn't anyone sitting on the platform, and everyone was standing around, looking mad. No one was painting.

Anna Patricia stood in the doorway with her hand on the latch. Suddenly a man with a beard pointed his finger at her and cried, "There! Let's get her."

Anna Patricia dropped the latch and ran. She ran as fast as she could go. She heard a man's voice calling after her, "Little girl! Little girl!"

Anna Patricia kept right on running until she reached the theater. She ran around the building to the stage door. She pushed against it. It would not open. She banged on it, but no one came. Anna Patricia's heart was beating very fast. Why didn't someone open the door? She pounded harder.

Suddenly she remembered that nobody was at the theater today. There was no one inside to open the door, no matter how hard she knocked. Anna Patricia's legs felt like macaroni—like cooked macaroni.

In a few minutes, when Anna Patricia had caught her breath, she decided to peep around the corner to see if the man with the beard was still in sight. She walked to the corner of the building and, keeping back against the wall, she looked around the edge of the building. What she saw made her draw back quickly. All of the artists were standing in a bunch by their door. They were all looking toward the theater. The man with the beard was pointing in Anna Patricia's direction.

Anna Patricia wished Eddie was with her. He would know what to do. She leaned against the wall, well out of sight. She was relieved that the artists were not following her. She decided to take another peep. Very slowly she stretched out her neck and took a look. What she saw made her jump, for the man with the beard was walking toward the theater. Each step was bringing him nearer.

Anna Patricia was scared. She didn't know what to do. She could only think of running, so Anna Patricia ran. She ran in the only direction she could run and not bump into the man with the beard. She ran behind the theater and behind some houses, through a garden and down to the rocks along the shore.

Anna Patricia could hear the man calling, "Little girl! Little girl!"

She kept to the rocks until she reached the rocks behind her own house. She saw Eddie on their dock and ran to him. "Oh, Eddie!" she gasped. "A man with a beard is after me."

"What did you do?" asked Eddie.

"I didn't do anything," said Anna Patricia. "I just looked in the door where the artists paint, and the man with the beard yelled at me. He yelled, 'Get her!' Then I ran, and everybody ran after me."

"Didn't I tell you not to stick your nose in there? You're too nosey, Annie Pat."

"I wasn't doing anything," said Anna Patricia. "I was just smelling the paint. I like the smell."

"You like the craziest things!" said Eddie.

"Let's go out in the sailboat, Eddie," said Anna Patricia. "That man with the beard may come down here. Let's go out in the sailboat."

Eddie was in bathing trunks. "I was just going to catch crabs," he said. "Do you want to catch crabs? I have two fish heads for bait."

"Oh, yes!" replied Anna Patricia. "Hurry up. Let's go."

"I have to go up to the house to get a basket and the fish heads. The fish heads are in the refrigerator," said Eddie, as he dashed off in the direction of the house.

"The net is here in the cockpit," Anna Patricia called after him.

"I know," Eddie called back.

"Hurry up!" cried Anna Patricia.

While Eddie was gone, Anna Patricia kept looking

out over the rocks she had just clambered over. She expected to see the man with the beard at any moment, but no one appeared.

It seemed ages before Eddie returned. When he did, he threw the basket into the cockpit. The fish heads were in the bottom of the basket wrapped up in a piece of newspaper.

Eddie unfastened the sailboat and jumped into the cockpit with Anna Patricia. They pushed off and sailed to a spot where they usually found crabs. There they dropped anchor.

Eddie tied one of the fish heads to a line for Anna Patricia. The other he tied to his own line.

Anna Patricia soon had a crab nibbling at her bait. "I've got one!" she said. "Quick, get the net."

Eddie reached down into the water with the net and scooped up the crab. He threw the crab into the basket. Another and another followed. The water around the sailboat was full of crabs.

The children caught crabs for over an hour. Anna Patricia was so excited that she forgot all about her escape from the artists and the man with the beard. At last the basket was almost full of crabs.

"Your mother will be glad when she sees all these crabs," said Eddie.

"Oh, yes!" said Anna Patricia. "And do I love crabs!"

"Me too," said Eddie. "This is a big mess of crabs."

Eddie pulled up the anchor, and they sailed back to their dock. He made the boat fast.

"Now, Annie Pat," he said, "help me with this basket. We have to lift it onto the dock. Take hold of the other handle, and be careful. We don't want to lose these crabs."

"I'll be careful," said Anna Patricia.

Anna Patricia took hold of one handle, and Eddie took hold of the other, and they lifted the basket of crabs. At the very moment that they lifted the basket,

131

a deep voice called out, "Here! Let me help you."

Anna Patricia looked up, and there, running toward them, was the man with the beard.

Anna Patricia dropped her side of the basket, and the crabs spilled out. They spilled into the water and they spilled into the cockpit. Anna Patricia turned and spilled herself right out of the sailboat. She dived right into the water in her new blue shorts and her new white blouse, and swam out to a raft, leaving Eddie with the man with the beard and the scratching, crawling crabs.

When she reached the raft, Anna Patricia climbed out of the water and lay down flat on her stomach. In a minute she lifted her head and looked back at the dock. She could see Eddie running to the house. The man with the beard stood on the dock looking down into the cockpit of the sailboat.

Anna Patricia watched. Now Eddie was running back again. He had the fire tongs from the fireplace in his hand. She couldn't see what was in his other hand, but Anna Patricia guessed that Eddie had gone to the house to get some things that could be used to pick up the crabs. Now Eddie and the man were in the cockpit. She was sure that they were getting the crabs back into the basket.

Anna Patricia didn't know what to do. She didn't know whether to stay where she was or to go back. She was afraid of the crabs now, too.

Soon she heard Eddie calling to her. "Hi! Annie Pat!" he called. "Come on in."

Anna Patricia decided to stay put.

In a few minutes Eddie dived into the water and swam out to the raft.

"That's the man who's after me," said Anna Patricia.

"Don't be so goosey!" said Eddie. "He isn't after you. He wants you to come to the art school and sit up on that platform. Those artists want to paint your picture. And, he's going to pay you just for sitting there."

"Pay me!" said Anna Patricia. "How much?"

"A dollar an hour!" said Eddie. "Three dollars every morning just for sitting still. Annie Pat, you've been running away from a lot of money."

Anna Patricia dived into the water and swam for home.

When she climbed out, the man with the beard said, "I've asked your mother if my students can paint your picture, and she says it's all right if you think you can sit still."

"What can I do while I'm sitting still?" Anna Patricia asked.

"What do you mean, what can you do?" asked the man.

"Well, I can sit stiller if I'm doing something," said Anna Patricia.

"Like what?" asked the man with the beard.

"Like doing a jigsaw puzzle maybe," replied Anna Patricia.

"Fine!" said the man.

So Anna Patricia went every morning to the art school, and the artists painted her picture while she worked on a big jigsaw puzzle.

When the children at the Children's Theater heard that Anna Patricia was getting a dollar an hour for working on a jigsaw puzzle, they all came and poked their heads in the door of the art school. They were all hoping to be asked to sit up on the platform and be paid for working on a jigsaw puzzle.

"It isn't as easy as you think," said Anna Patricia to Eddie one day, when she came home from the art class. "Sometimes my foot goes to sleep! And if I scratch my nose, somebody says, 'Please don't scratch your nose. I'm painting your nose.'"

"Well, sure!" said Eddie. "You get paid for sitting still, not for scratching your nose."

135

"But if it itches, it itches!" said Anna Patricia, as she stuck three more dollars into her bank.

The following week the man with the beard asked Eddie to sit on the platform. The artists all wanted to paint Eddie. Eddie was delighted. All he had to do was sit still and read a book.

What did Eddie discover? His foot went to sleep. His nose itched. His ear itched. His neck itched. His chin itched. He agreed with Anna Patricia that it was not as easy as it looked, but they both liked making so much money and feeling so rich.

Anna Patricia said, "It's wonderful! I don't know which I like best, to paint or to be painted. I guess I just like to do what I'm doing—whatever I'm doing, that is. Of course, if I'm making money doing what I'm doing, that's wonderful. I never made any money painting, so I guess I like being painted best. But then, I never had any of those nice gooey paints, so I don't really know."

CHAPTER 8

THE HURRICANE

Davey loved the sea gulls. He loved to watch them as they circled above the water. He watched them swoop down and pick up little white clam shells, fly up high with them in their beaks, and then drop them onto the rocks below. The clam would fall with a crack that broke it open and then, quick as a flash, the gull would skim down and eat the soft clam from the shell. This went on all day long. Crack! Crack! Crack! Davey wondered how the gulls could eat so many clams.

One morning Davey had run down to the little dock before breakfast. In a few minutes he was back. He rushed into the kitchen crying, "Get out the sneakbox! Get out the sneakbox! There are ducks! Ducks!"

"Davey!" said Eddie. "There aren't any ducks around here. They're all sea gulls. You know they're sea gulls. Don't be silly!"

"But these are ducks!" shouted Davey.

"Let's go see," said Anna Patricia.

"You know there are no ducks around here, Annie Pat," said Eddie, as Anna Patricia and Davey ran out of the kitchen.

But in a minute Anna Patricia and Davey were back. "They *are* ducks!" Anna Patricia cried. "Can we have some bread to feed them, Mother?"

"They can't fly up and crack clams," said Davey. "We have to feed them."

Anna Patricia's mother gave the children some slices of bread, and Davey and Anna Patricia and Eddie went back to the dock. "See, Eddie," said Anna Patricia, "they are ducks."

"Sure enough!" said Eddie.

The children broke the bread into pieces and threw the pieces to the ducks. Davey laughed each time one of the ducks put his head in the water and stuck his tail and his back feet up in the air.

"We wouldn't sneak up on these ducks and shoot them, would we?" said Davey.

"Oh, no!" said Anna Patricia.

"I'd like to sneak up on those sea gulls," said Eddie, as he watched one of them snatch up a piece of bread and fly away with it.

"Go eat clams!" Davey shouted at the sea gulls.

The ducks swam around, occasionally saying, "Quack! Quack!"

"I'm glad we use the sneakbox for a sailboat," said

Davey. "I don't know how anybody could use it to shoot those ducks."

"They're so pretty!" said Anna Patricia. "I hope they stay here."

Later in the day the children decided to take the sailboat out. Eddie put up the sail. Anna Patricia was crew, and Davey was passenger in his bright orange life jacket. The ducks were paddling near the dock.

As the wind filled the sail, the boat began to move forward. Then, to the children's great surprise, the three ducks swam along with the sailboat, one behind the other.

"Oh, look!" said Davey. "The ducks are coming with us."

The children laughed at the ducks, and so did everyone else who saw them. The ducks followed the boat until it picked up speed and left them behind.

The children sailed for an hour. On their way back, as they neared their dock, there were the three ducks.

They looked as though they were watching for the return of the sailboat. Sure enough, they followed the sailboat back into port, like three little tugboats beside an ocean liner.

The ducks stayed on, and the children fed them every day. Every time the children took the sailboat out, the ducks played follow-the-leader. They always went the same distance. When the sailboat returned, there were the ducks apparently waiting for the children. The ducks had adopted the children as much as the children had adopted the ducks.

One day, near the end of the summer, the children awoke to a rainy day instead of sunshine. As the day wore on, it grew darker and darker. Over the radio there were warnings of a hurricane. It was coming up the coast.

"What's a hurricane?" Davey asked his Aunt Mary.

"It's very heavy rain and a lot of wind," she replied. "We must do whatever they tell us to do over the radio."

Everyone took the rigging off his sailboat and put it in a safe place. The *Ladybug* was tied securely to the dock, and Dr. Wallace hoped it would hold through the storm.

Everyone in the town fastened awnings securely. Windows were boarded up as if for the winter. Swinging signboards were taken down. Everything that could be carried inside was put under cover.

Late in the morning it began to blow, and it rained harder and harder. The wind blew like something alive. It whistled around the corners of the houses and bent the tree trunks as though they were made of rubber. Great white waves broke over the rocks, each one coming closer to the houses built on the shore.

Anna Patricia's father had boarded up the windows on the harbor side of the house, but the children could hear the angry sea.

"Those waves hitting the rocks sound like somebody shooting," said Eddie.

"The poor sailboat!" said Anna Patricia.

"The poor ducks!" said Davey.

At three o'clock in the afternoon, a message came over the radio, telling everyone who lived along the shore to come to the high school as quickly as possible. Eddie and Anna Patricia and Davey thought this was very exciting. They kept telling each other that they were not scared, as they watched Anna Patricia's mother pack a suitcase with things that they would need for the night.

Dr. and Mrs. Wallace and the children put on slickers and rain hats and ran out to the car. The road in front of the house was already a rushing stream.

"This is real exciting!" said Eddie from the back seat of the car, where the children were sitting.

"Oh, look at the blue fire and sparks coming from those wires," Davey cried, pointing to some electric wires that had fallen down.

"We have to be careful of those," said Dr. Wallace.

145

The high school was built on a high cliff, safe from the sea. It was not very far from the Wallaces' house, but it took them a long time to get to it, because of the electric wires that were crackling and sputtering in the streets. Some streets were blocked with trees that had been blown down.

Anna Patricia's father tried one street after another. Finally, they found one that was clear of both wires and trees, and they drove into the school parking lot. Many cars were already parked there.

"I hope we get something to eat," said Davey.

"I'm sure we shall," said Mrs. Wallace. "I have some cans of soup right here in this shopping bag, and two loaves of bread, and milk and butter. We'll be all right."

"I don't like cold soup," said Davey.

"Don't worry!" said his Aunt Mary. "There's a kitchen in the school, with more than one stove, too."

"Anyway," said Anna Patricia, "you shouldn't be

146

thinking just about yourself, Davey. You should be thinking of saving people's lives."

"I hope everybody's life gets saved," said Davey. "And I hope our ducks get saved."

"The poor ducks!" said Anna Patricia.

"I hope the sailboat gets saved," said Eddie.

"It isn't alive!" said Davey.

"I know that," said Eddie, "but I don't want it smashed up."

Many families had left their homes and were now safe inside the high school. Some of the bigger boys were playing basketball in the gymnasium. Some of the girls were dancing square dances on the stage in the auditorium.

Davey joined a group of children who were listening to a mother reading a story book. Eddie and Anna Patricia followed her mother to the school kitchen. There, big kettles of soup were steaming on a stove.

They each had a bowl of delicious fish chowder. Later Davey ate two bowls of it.

The storm raged all afternoon. When it grew dark they found there were no electric lights anywhere in the school. Many people had brought candles, and they lighted them. Anna Patricia said it looked like Christmas, with the candles in the windows.

Everyone was fed, and soon the children were asleep on blankets. Fathers and mothers whispered together while great gusts of rain lashed at the windows.

Anna Patricia woke up in the middle of the night. It was very dark and quiet. Everyone seemed to be asleep. She looked up. She could see out of one of the big windows. At first she thought she saw the flame of a candle, but soon she realized that she was looking at a bright star in the sky. The storm was all over. Anna Patricia went back to sleep.

In the morning everyone hurried to get back to their homes. It wasn't easy because of the fallen trees and wires, but the Wallaces, with Eddie and Davey, reached home at last.

The children ran to the back porch to see if they could see the sailboat. To their surprise, they heard, "Quack! Quack! Quack!"

All three children looked over the railing. The water was as high as the porch floor and there, paddling around, were the three ducks. "Quack! Quack! Quack!"

"Oh! The poor little things!" exclaimed Anna Patricia. "They must be starved."

Anna Patricia got some bread, and she and Davey threw pieces to the ducks.

Eddie's eyes were searching for the sailboat. All the rocks were covered with water, and waves rolled over them. At last he saw something white that didn't break into spray. He ran and got Dr. Wallace's binoculars. He looked through them and saw the bottom of a sailboat.

Eddie pointed to it and said. "There's a sailboat. I hope it's the *Ladybug*."

"Oh, I hope so!" said Anna Patricia, taking the glasses from Eddie. "I hope it's the *Ladybug!*" She ran into the house and called to her father. "Daddy!" she called out. "We've found the ducks, and we think we have found the *Ladybug!*"

Dr. Wallace came out on the porch and took the glasses from Eddie.

Eddie pointed to what he thought was the *Ladybug*. "See!" he said. "Right over there."

Dr. Wallace looked in the direction Eddie pointed. "It's a sailboat," he said, "bottom side up."

"Do you think it's the *Ladybug?*" said Anna Patricia.

"Just a minute," said her father. "I'm trying to see the name on it."

The children huddled close to Dr. Wallace, while he kept the glasses leveled on the sailboat. The waves

broke over it and pulled back into the sea one after another. The tide was going out, and more and more of the sailboat could be seen.

Suddenly Anna Patricia's father said, "It *is* the *Ladybug!* I can see the name now. It's the *Ladybug!*"

"It's the *Ladybug!* It's the *Ladybug!*" the three children cried out in chorus.

CHAPTER 9

WILLY THE SEA URCHIN

WHEN the floods of water were gone, Dr. Wallace and Eddie and Anna Patricia went to inspect the sailboat. They were delighted to find that there was very little damage. It was badly scratched, but Anna Patricia's father said, "With a fresh coat of paint, it will look like new."

"Come on, Annie Pat," said Eddie, "let's explore.

Maybe a lot of valuable property was washed in with that big storm."

"Well, if we find any, we have to divide it," said Anna Patricia, "and we have to give something to Davey."

"O.K.!" said Eddie.

The children were in their bathing suits. They ran over the rocks and were surprised to find great heavy pieces of timber washed up on them.

"I'll bet these logs were part of a wreck," said Eddie.

"Well, if there was a wreck," said Anna Patricia, "there should be lots of things beside logs."

"Sure!" said Eddie. "We just have to keep looking."

Anna Patricia went down to the water's edge, where pools lay between the rocks. In a few moments she called out, "Oh, Eddie, here is the most wonderful flower. It must be something from the bottom of the ocean, or maybe it's a sea urchin."

Eddie came leaping over the rocks. "What's a sea urchin?" he asked.

"Oh, it's a sort of an animal that lives in the ocean," said Anna Patricia. "I'm sure this is one. It's beautiful!"

Anna Patricia pointed down into the water, and Eddie stooped over. He looked down at something white that was floating there. It was long and hollow and hung down into the water. Its outer edges were curled over.

"I think it's some kind of a lily," said Eddie.

"Oh, no," said Anna Patricia. "It isn't a lily. It's a sea urchin, and we should put it in an aquarium and keep it. Then we can take it home with us and take it to school. It's a real treasure."

"I guess you're right, Annie Pat," said Eddie. "I'll go and get a bucket and scoop it up. You watch it so it doesn't get away." Anna Patricia watched until Eddie returned with the bucket.

"I think we should name it," said Anna Patricia. "Everything alive should have a name."

156

"How can you name it?" asked Eddie. "You don't know whether it's a boy urchin or a girl urchin."

"You said it looked like a lily," said Anna Patricia, "so let's name it Lily."

"But maybe it's a boy sea urchin," said Eddie. "No boy would want to be called Lily."

"Well then, let's call it Willy. Then if it is a girl sea urchin, her name can be Willimina, and Willy would be her nickname."

Eddie stopped down with the bucket and scooped up Willy.

"Oh, Eddie!" said Anna Patricia. "What do you suppose we should feed it?"

"Oh, I guess it eats that fish food that looks like white paper, or maybe seaweed."

"I hope so," said Anna Patricia. "I wouldn't want it to starve to death."

"Maybe we'll have to try different things," said Eddie.

Eddie and Anna Patricia were looking down at Willy when Davey came running over the rocks. "What have you got in the bucket?" he called out.

"We have a sea urchin," Anna Patricia answered.

"Is it alive?" said Davey.

"Of course," said Anna Patricia.

"Let me look," said Davey.

Eddie and Anna Patricia made way for Davey to look into the bucket.

"That's a funny thing," said Davey. "What does it do?"

"What do you mean, 'What does it do?'" replied Eddie.

"Well, everything alive does something," said Davey.

"It floats," said Anna Patricia.

Davey continued to bend over the bucket. Suddenly he said, "Do you know? It looks like a sock."

Eddie looked again. "Sort of," he said.

"I think it *is* a sock," said Davey.

158

"Don't be silly!" said Anna Patricia.

"Well, I'm going to poke it with this stick," said Davey.

"Don't you dare!" cried Anna Patricia. "You might hurt it."

"Annie Pat," said Eddie, "it does look like a sock. It looks like a white sock with a hole in the toe."

Davey poked his stick into the bucket. "Be careful!" said Anna Patricia.

Davey caught what had just been named Willy on the stick and lifted an old white woolen sock out of the bucket. Eddie laughed and laughed. He pointed to the dripping sock. "Look at Annie Pat's Willy!" he cried.

Anna Patricia and Davey laughed and laughed.

"Annie Pat," said Eddie, "you get the craziest ideas! A sea urchin! Willy! Just somebody's old sock!"

"Willimina!" said Anna Patricia, and went into another spasm of laughing.

"Well, let's keep Willimina," said Eddie. "Maybe we can fool all of our friends over at the theater." He carried the bucket to a safe spot and set it down.

"Let's explore some more," said Anna Patricia. "Maybe we'll find something else."

The three children went from rock to rock. Sometimes they walked in the water. The stones were very slippery there. Finally they came to a large rock. They climbed over it, and there on the other side, half in the water and half out, was a small trunk with a rounded lid. It had rusty iron bands and rusty hinges. The lock was rusted too.

Eddie's mouth fell open. Then he said in an awed voice, "A treasure chest!"

"Pirates!" said Anna Patricia. "Maybe there's gold inside."

"If there are any gold pennies, can I have them?" said Davey. "I collect shiny pennies."

Eddie was already in the water trying to lift the

trunk. "Help me with this, Annie Pat," he said. "This is real treasure."

Anna Patricia got into the water, and together they pulled at the trunk. The rocks were so slippery that Anna Patricia kept losing her footing and falling into the water.

"Annie Pat," said Eddie, "get your feet into the pebbles, or we shall never get this chest where we can open it."

Anna Patricia pushed her feet down into the pebbles and pulled at the trunk. Finally she and Eddie got the trunk onto the dry rock.

Eddie examined the lock. It was broken, but the rust held it shut. He picked up a small rock and beat on the lock. He beat it, and he beat it.

Anna Patricia and Davey watched. They were both wondering what would be inside. Anna Patricia was beginning to think that Eddie would never get the chest open when, suddenly, the lock came loose.

Eddie pulled at the lid, and Anna Patricia and Davey knelt down to look inside. The hinges creaked as Eddie tugged at the lid. He pushed and he pulled. At last he raised the lid so that the children could see inside.

The first thing Eddie lifted out of the trunk was a toy fire engine covered with rust. He examined it and said, "This will be O.K. when it's painted."

"Can I have it?" Davey asked.

"Maybe," said Eddie.

Then he handed a large round tin box to Anna Patricia. Anna Patricia shook it. It rattled. "Oh, maybe this is full of gold!" she said.

The last thing Eddie took out of the trunk was a bag filled with something that made lumps all over it.

"Oh, Eddie," said Davey, when he saw the bag, "do you think that is a bag of gold?"

"I don't know what it is," said Eddie.

Anna Patricia was tugging at the lid of the box.

164

She couldn't budge it. "Oh, Eddie," she said, "get this lid off. Try the rock. See if you can get the lid off. I'm just crazy to see what's inside."

Eddie took the box and began to beat around the edge of the lid with the rock. It didn't do much good.

"Oh, here!" said Anna Patricia. "Let me do it."

"You just asked *me* to do it," said Eddie.

"Well, you're too slow," said Anna Patricia.

Anna Patricia beat on the edges of the lid with the rock, while Eddie tried to undo some rusty wire that held the bag shut. Suddenly the lid of the box flew off and fell down on the rocks. A shower of buttons tumbled out. They bounced and rolled every which way down into the shallow water at the edge of the rocks.

"Now look, Annie Pat!" said Eddie. "Why do you have to go and make such a mess of everything?"

These words were just out of Eddie's mouth, when

the wire he was working on broke and a shower of marbles clattered down and followed the buttons into the water.

"Now we don't have anything but the fire engine," said Davey.

"I'm going to get those buttons," said Anna Patricia. "I can see them."

"Come on, Davey," said Eddie, "help me get the marbles. They're swell marbles. I'll give you half of them."

The children spent the rest of the afternoon picking up buttons and marbles. Fortunately, the tide was out, and that made it easier.

When they had gathered all they could find, Anna Patricia said, "These are the most beautiful buttons I ever saw."

"What are you going to do with them?" Eddie asked.

"I haven't decided yet," said Anna Patricia, "but

I'll think of something. What are you going to do with your marbles?"

"Play marbles, of course," said Eddie.

"Oh, I'm going to do something with my buttons that nobody ever did with buttons before," said Anna Patricia. "I haven't thought of anything yet, but I will."

"I bet you will!" said Eddie.

CHAPTER 10

THE YOU-SEE-'EM

Anna Patricia, Eddie, and Davey carried their treasures over the rocks and into the house. Davey carried the rusty fire engine. Eddie and Anna Patricia carried the old trunk between them, with the bag of marbles and the button box inside. Eddie also carried Willy in the bucket in his other hand.

"I guess these things should go in a 'you-see-'em,' " said Davey.

"It isn't a 'you-see-'em,' Davey," said Anna Patricia. "It's a museum."

"Well, you see 'em, don't you?" said Davey.

"Davey is right," said Eddie. "I think 'you-see-'em' is a much better name than museum."

"I'll tell you, Eddie!" said Anna Patricia. "Let's have a 'you-see-'em' on our back porch."

"We don't have enough things to show," said Eddie.

Anna Patricia laughed. "Willy is important enough," she said.

"I think I saw a big aquarium in the garage," said Eddie. "We can put Willy in that. We can fool people."

The children deposited their treasures on the back porch. Then they went to the garage to look for the aquarium that Eddie thought was there. They soon found it. It was covered with cobwebs, and a corner was broken off at the top.

171

"This is wonderful," said Eddie. "It will hold water, and Willy will look real when we put him inside."

"We must put some seaweed in, too," said Anna Patricia. "I'll go find some seaweed."

Anna Patricia dashed off for seaweed. By the time she returned, Eddie had washed the aquarium. Anna Patricia put the seaweed in, and Eddie dumped Willy in.

"No one will ever guess that Willy is a sock," said Anna Patricia. "We should put up a sign, *Come see Willy, the sea urchin.*"

"Maybe other people have found things that were washed up in the hurricane," said Eddie. "Maybe they'd like to show them in our 'you-see-'em.' "

"Why don't you make a sign?" said Anna Patricia. "We could put it up on the outside of the theater. Then everybody could bring their treasures and show them in our 'you-see-'em.' "

"O.K.," said Eddie.

There was nothing Eddie liked better than making signs. He set to work the next morning. He found a sheet of brown cardboard that would do very nicely for a sign. With some black paint he painted the letters.

When Eddie finished, the sign said,

EXBISHUN
BRING YOUR HURRY CANE TREASURES
TO THE WALLACES YOU-SEE-'EM
COME SEE WILLY THE SEA URCHIN

While Eddie painted the sign, Anna Patricia went over all of her buttons. She laid out some bright yellow ones so that they looked like the petals of a flower and put a brown button in the center.

"Oh look, Eddie!" she cried. "Look! I made a black-eyed Susan out of these buttons!"

"Don't bother me," said Eddie. "I'm busy."

Anna Patricia looked down at the sign that Eddie

was painting on the floor and said, "You don't have that word *exhibition* spelled right."

"How do you spell it?" asked Eddie.

"Well, I know it has an *h* in it," said Anna Patricia.

"I've got an *h* in it," said Eddie.

"It isn't in the right place," said Anna Patricia. "You have it near the end, and it comes near the beginning. The *u* is in the wrong place, too."

"You know so much!" said Eddie. "You spell it."

"E-x-h-u-b-i-s-o-n," Anna Patricia replied.

"I don't believe it," said Eddie. "That doesn't sound like a word."

"Eddie, you know you've made some terrible mistakes on signs before. You don't want everybody around here to think you're a dummy."

"I'm not a dummy!" said Eddie. "Just to show you that I'm right and you're wrong, Annie Pat, I'll look in the dictionary."

Eddie went into the house and found the dictionary.

He opened it and ran his finger up and down the columns of words until he found *exhibition*. He copied it on a piece of paper.

When he returned to the porch, Anna Patricia said, "Well?"

"You were wrong," said Eddie.

"Well!" said Anna Patricia.

"It's a little different from mine, too," Eddie said.

"Ha!" said Anna Patricia. "Didn't I tell you?"

"You didn't tell me right," said Eddie.

"Well, I told you, anyway," said Anna Patricia.

"Annie Pat, you're all scrambled up," said Eddie. "I never knew anybody who could get as scrambled up as you."

"Is that so?" said Anna Patricia. "If I hadn't told you, you would have looked like a dummy."

Eddie sat on the floor trying to decide how he could correct the word *exhibition*. He finally decided to cover the word with white paint and start over again.

Anna Patricia sat at the table making flowers out of her buttons. Suddenly an idea came to her. "Do you know what, Eddie?" she said.

"What?" replied Eddie.

"I'm going to paint a picture with these buttons," Anna Patricia answered.

"Annie Pat," said Eddie, "you can't paint a picture with buttons. You tried to paint a picture with jam and marmalade and toothpaste and catchup, and you know you made an awful mess. You can't paint a picture with buttons."

"Well, not exactly paint," said Anna Patricia, "but I'm going to make a picture of flowers with these buttons."

"It will be another Annie-Pat mess," said Eddie.

"It will not," said Anna Patricia. "It will be beautiful. I'm going to get a piece of cloth and sew button flowers all over it."

Anna Patricia ran off to get a piece of cloth from

178

her mother. The only cloth her mother could give her was a piece of sack that had been brought from home with potatoes in it.

Anna Patricia was soon at work. Eddie left her to take his sign over to the theater where he tacked it on the outside wall.

With a crayon Anna Patricia marked on the piece of potato sacking. She marked the place for the flowers, the stems, and the leaves.

Her mother looked over her shoulder and said, "I'll give you some green wool for the stems."

"I guess I'd better make the stems first," said Anna Patricia.

Her mother gave her the wool, and Anna Patricia stitched in the stems. The rest of the day she spent sewing buttons on in the form of flowers. The next morning she sewed green buttons on for leaves.

When she finished, Eddie said, "What are you going to do with it?"

"I'm going to put it in that frame I have and hang it up in the 'you-see-'em.' "

Just then Jim and Debbie and Christie arrived. They had an express wagon filled with the things they had found after the hurricane. They had found several bottles. One had a note in it giving the date it had been thrown into the ocean. Jim had found an oar, and Christie had found a big sponge.

"Come see our sea urchin!" said Eddie.

"Oh, yes!" said Anna Patricia. "Just wait until you see our sea urchin. We named it Willy, but maybe it's Willimina. Anyway, it's Willy for sure."

Jim and Debbie and Christie gathered around the aquarium. They all looked down at Willy. Finally Jim said, "Where is it?"

"Where is what?" asked Anna Patricia.

"The sea urchin," Jim replied.

"You're looking at it," said Anna Patricia.

Jim pointed to Willy and said, "You mean that thing?"

"Willy is not a thing," said Anna Patricia. "Willy is a sea urchin."

"Anna Patricia!" said Jim. "I hate to tell you, but Willy is a sock."

Debbie and Christie laughed and laughed. "A sea urchin! A sea urchin!" they giggled.

"But doesn't it look like a sea urchin?" asked Anna Patricia.

"Not to me," said Jim. "It looks just like a sock."

"It looks just like a sock to me, too," said Debbie.

"I'd never think it was a sea urchin," said Christie.

"Well, I'm glad it looks like a sea urchin to me," said Anna Patricia. "It's much more fun to see a sea urchin than an old sock."

"That's right, Annie Pat," said Eddie. "It was fun down on the rocks when you found it and thought it was a sea urchin."

The children set to work arranging their treasures, and soon the "you-see-'em" was set up. Anna Patricia hung up her button picture.

"I don't think it belongs in this exhibition," said Debbie, "because it wasn't washed up in the hurricane."

"The buttons were," said Anna Patricia. "It doesn't make any difference whether the buttons are lying on the table or hanging on the wall."

"That's right," said Eddie. "Buttons are buttons."

"O.K.," said Christie, "but I think it's a very peculiar thing to do with buttons."

"Not if you like to do it," said Anna Patricia.

Over the week end boys and girls and some grown-ups dropped in to look at the things in the "you-see-'em." They all laughed over Willy, and they all said things like, "Well, I never!" and "What a thing!" when they saw Anna Patricia's button picture.

On Sunday afternoon the artist whom Eddie and Anna Patricia had watched, while she painted the picture that didn't look like a boat, came to the "you-see-'em." When she saw Anna Patricia's flower picture, she exclaimed, "How wonderful! I must have this beautiful picture. Would you sell it to me for five dollars?"

"Oh, yes!" said Anna Patricia. "I have lots of buttons. I can make another one."

The artist left with the button picture under her arm. Anna Patricia smoothed out her five crisp, new dollar bills.

"Annie Pat," said Eddie, "sometimes I think you sound like an awful dummy, but I like being with you."

"Do you, Eddie?" said Anna Patricia.

"Yes, I do," replied Eddie, "because you see all kinds of things. You see sea urchins instead of socks, flowers instead of buttons, and paint instead of jam, toothpaste, and mustard."

"It's more fun if you do," said Anna Patricia.

"You bet," said Eddie.

185

CAROLYN HAYWOOD is distinguished both as author and illustrator of children's books. Her first book was published in 1939. Since then she has had many other books published and has become one of the most widely read American writers for younger children.

Carolyn Haywood was born in Philadelphia and still lives in that city. She is a graduate of the Philadelphia Normal School and studied at the Pennsylvania Academy of Fine Arts, where she won the Cresson European Scholarship for distinguished work. Miss Haywood calls herself a "grand-pupil" of the great American illustrator, Howard Pyle, having studied with three of his distinguished pupils, Elizabeth Shippen Green Elliott, Violet Oakley, and Jessie Willcox Smith. She is also a portrait painter and has specialized in portraits of children. Her experience in this field has given her a sympathetic understanding of children and their interests which has made her peculiarly well fitted to write and illustrate for them. She is continuing her portrait work with commissions in New York, Philadelphia, and other eastern cities.

Miss Haywood has published 21 books, all of which she has illustrated herself.

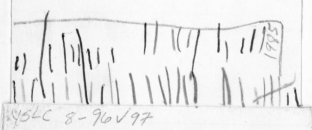